Beating the
DROUGHT

Diana Noonan

illustrated by Jenny Cooper

Learning Media

Chapter 1

"That's it!" said Mom, gazing at the television. "Everyone has to share the bathwater."

"Yuck!" groaned Pete and Melanie.
"We're not sharing bathwater with
anyone."

"Same," I mumbled.

"Listen up!" said Mom. She switched off
the TV and looked at us hard. "You
heard what they said." She waved a
finger at the TV screen. "We're in the
middle of a really bad drought. We have
to save water – all of us."

Grandpa was sitting on the other side of the room. He shuffled about in his chair.

"And you can't water the garden," Mom said. "Do you all understand? You can be fined if you get caught." She looked suddenly at Grandpa, but he was hiding behind the newspaper.

"No one is to use the garden hose or the sprinkler. The plants will have to do their bit too."

Melanie giggled. She's only six, but she knew that Mom was really talking about Grandpa's pumpkin patch. It was in for a hard time!

Chapter 2

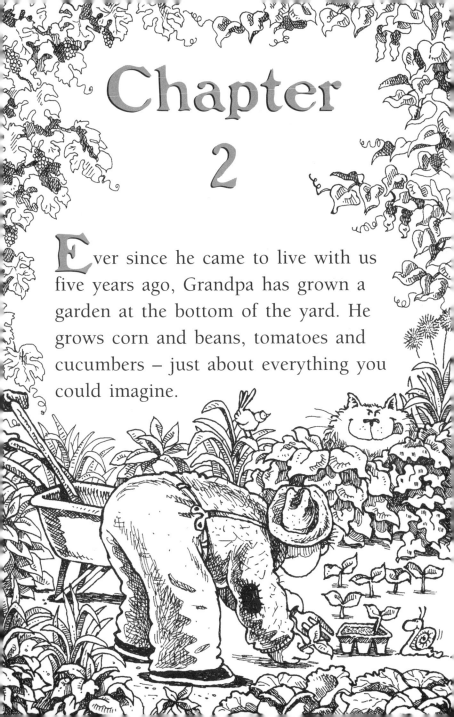

Ever since he came to live with us five years ago, Grandpa has grown a garden at the bottom of the yard. He grows corn and beans, tomatoes and cucumbers – just about everything you could imagine.

But the thing that grows best is his pumpkin vine. Every year at the local garden show, he's won first prize for the largest pumpkin. He tells everyone that the secret is water. Lots of water at the right time.

But if water was the secret, then his pumpkin was in big trouble this year. At least, that's what we thought. Grandpa had other ideas!

That night, we threw dice to see who got the first bath. When we'd all finished, Mom soaked Pete's baseball uniform in the same water. Then the water went into the washing machine.

When Mom went to pull the plug to let the cold, gray scum out of the tub, she found Grandpa standing behind her. He was carrying two plastic buckets. "Leave the water right there," he said. "I need it for the garden."

That was the beginning of Grandpa's project.

Chapter 3

For the next few weeks while the pumpkin fruit was starting to grow, Grandpa poured all the used water from the house onto the plant. When the greasy, gray dishwater was cold, he scooped it out of the sink with a bowl and carried it outside.

He began washing his socks in a bucket and poured that water onto the pumpkin patch too. He even paid us kids to clean our teeth in a mug in the garden so that he could use the slops!

Then Grandpa did something that was a shock to all of us. Mom usually had to *make* Grandpa take a bath every Sunday. But he started having his weekly bath without being asked. Mom soon put a stop to that!

Grandpa's watering project went on late
into the summer. By then, he'd chosen
one pumpkin to win the prize. But it was
growing so big that all the used water
from the house wasn't enough for it.

One day when we came home from school, Mom told us that Grandpa had been over to the neighbors' house with his buckets!

I was so embarrassed. I couldn't even talk to the Singhs anymore!

Nothing we said could keep Grandpa
from watering that pumpkin, and he
didn't stop at the neighbors'. He went
right around the block, from door to
door, asking for wastewater.

One day at school, I heard some teachers talking about Grandpa. And they were looking at me! But no matter what we said, Grandpa kept right on collecting water and feeding the pumpkin. It swelled larger and larger and started to turn bright orange.

Chapter

4

About a week before the first frost in October, I saw a notice about the garden show in the window of our supermarket, and I knew it wouldn't be long before Grandpa cut his prize pumpkin from its vine.

When I arrived home the next afternoon, Grandpa was in the kitchen. He was sharpening his pocketknife on the stone he keeps in his pocket.

He looked up at me very seriously. "Fetch the wheelbarrow, there's a good lad," he said.

When we got to the garden, Grandpa walked round and round his champion pumpkin. He looked at it this way and that. He rubbed his thumb up and down his chin. Then he stepped across the garden, parted the pumpkin leaves, and began cutting.

It took Grandpa and me ages to roll the pumpkin up two strong pieces of wood and into the wheelbarrow. Grandpa pushed it, little by little, until it was finally in place. The barrow looked as if it might topple over under the weight.

Grandpa pushed the barrow across the grass and over to the garage. He opened the car trunk and looked over at the pumpkin. "Now, then," he said. "In you go."

Together, we moved the huge pumpkin into the trunk. "Right," Grandpa said to the pumpkin. "Tomorrow morning, you're off to the show!"

Chapter 5

Usually, Mom takes us all to the garden show. But this year, after Grandpa had embarrassed us by collecting water from our neighbors, we didn't really feel like going. Grandpa didn't seem to care. For hours, he fussed about, putting on his suit and polishing his shoes.

Grandpa kept looking at his watch. He
muttered about the weather. "A warm day
isn't good for weighing pumpkins," he
said. Then he gave me a secret wink and
drove off in his car.

None of us was surprised when he came home later that day, whistling and smiling. Pinned onto his hat was a red ribbon.

"There we are," said Grandpa, passing a bright "first place" certificate to Melanie.

We gathered round to look at it.

"Were there many pumpkins this year?" asked Mom.

"Not as many as last year," said Grandpa.

"Something to do with the weather, I suppose," said Mom, a smile twitching at the corner of her lips.

I held my hand over my mouth to stop myself laughing.

"Well," said Mom, "you deserve that prize more than ever, Grandpa, because you worked so hard for the water."

Then she looked at us. "Homework time, everyone," she said. "And I want you all at the dinner table at six o'clock sharp. We're having a very special meal tonight."

Mom is a really great cook, so I couldn't
wait to see what she'd fixed for dinner.
My stomach rumbled as I sat down at the
table and watched her put down a big,
steaming saucepan.

She took off the lid, and a rich, spicy smell wafted out. We all leaned over to look into the saucepan.

"I've made Grandpa's prize-winning pumpkin into soup," said Mom. "Doesn't it smell delicious?"

Grandpa grinned. He looked so proud that I thought he was going to burst. "There'll be plenty more pumpkin where that came from," he said, holding out his plate.

That was when I began to feel sick.

Tiny sprigs of parsley floated in the creamy, orange soup, but all I saw swimming in front of me was gray bathwater, sock juice, and toothpaste slops – not just ours but the whole street's!

"Actually," I said, "I'm not feeling hungry tonight."

Mom must have known exactly what I was thinking because as Grandpa started slurping his soup at the end of the table, she winked at me and smiled.

"I've made tomato soup too," she grinned, "just in case pumpkin doesn't happen to agree with anyone!"